The Lost Diary of Shakespeare's
Ghostwriter

The Lost Diary of Shakespeare's Ghostwriter

**Discovered by Steve Barlow
and Steve Skidmore**

Illustrated by George Hollingworth

Collins
An imprint of HarperCollins*Publishers*

First published in Great Britain by Collins in 1999

Collins is an imprint of HarperCollins*Publishers* Ltd,
77-85 Fulham Palace Road, Hammersmith, London W6 8JB

The HarperCollins website address is
www.**fire**and**water**.com

3 5 7 9 8 6 4

Text copyright © Steve Barlow and Steve Skidmore 1999
Illustrations copyright © George Hollingworth 1999
Cover illustration copyright © Martin Chatterton 1999

ISBN 0 00 694588 0

The authors assert the moral right to be
identified as the authors of the work.

Printed and bound in Great Britain by
Caledonian International Book Manufacturing Ltd, Glasgow, G64

MESSAGE TO READERS

Was William Shakespeare, the Bard, the Swan of Avon, really England's greatest ever playwright?

Was he the genius who wrote *Hamlet, King Lear* and *Romeo and Juliet*? It seems the answer is…

NO!

This 'Lost Diary' explodes the myth of the man from Stratford in the biggest bombshell ever to hit the world of literature! In his diary, Eggbert Noah Bacon (a character previously unknown to historians) makes the astonishing claim that it was actually *he* who wrote Shakespeare's plays!

Barlow and Skidmore claim to have found Eggbert's diary in the cellars beneath The Globe. (Although when pressed, they admitted that the Globe in question was not the great theatre of Shakespeare's day, now reconstructed on the south bank of the River Thames in London, but a public house in Birmingham.)

Early entries reveal that the half-brother of Francis Bacon (famous writer, philosopher and statesman), had an unhappy childhood. He was bullied at school and was given the nickname "Streaky". However, by far the most interesting part of the diary is that dealing with the partnership between him and William Shakespeare; and it is this section that is presented here.

Can Eggbert's astounding claim be true?

Read what follows and judge for yourselves…

Alas the day! What will become of me?

Oh that I, Eggbert Noah Bacon, son of Sir Nicholas Bacon, half-brother of Francis Bacon, should have come to this.

I have just read the latest letter from my father. In it, he says that he is disgusted by my drinking, gambling, extravagance and idleness. He is stopping my allowance and refusing to pay my debts! He says he will cut me off without a groat*… or it could be "without a goat", his handwriting is absolutely dreadful.

What can I do? I owe money all over London. Some of the people I owe money to have very long swords and very short tempers.

In fact, there is only one thing a decent, self-respecting gentleman can do at times like these…

Run away!

*A small coin, worth fourpence in Elizabethan money.

9th September, 1589

I've been lying low in the country at Pinky Hartington's house, in Kelston. He's an old school chum of mine, and more than happy to have me as a house guest.

However, I'm wishing I hadn't bothered! The rest of the country is still rejoicing in our victory over the Spanish but all *he* does is drone on endlessly about his new invention; an indoor privy, if you please.

"But won't it be terribly stinky, Pinky?" I asked him.

He said no, that was the clever bit.

Then he insisted on showing me the plans:

Tank of fresh water.

Seat on which to place botty.

Water flushes smelly bits down pipe.

Pooh! Pooh! Pooh!

What a disgusting, ridiculous contraption! It'll never catch on.

A band of strolling players turned up in the local inn today to perform *The Spanish Tragedy*, a play by Mr Thomas Kyd. It's still very popular because of the defeat of the Spanish Armada.*

I had nothing better to do, so I toddled along. At half time, while I was in the Gents', just buttoning my codpiece, I heard a cry of, "Streaky Bacon! What are *you* doing here?"

I turned round, and there was Inky Shakespeare, a chap who had been at school with me back in Stratford. Apparently he was acting in the play, but I hadn't recognised him because he was wearing a wig and he had grown a silly moustache (and there was a ladder in his tights).

* The battle against the Spanish Armada was fought on 30th July, 1588. Spain had declared war on England because:
• Francis Drake's ships kept raiding Spanish treasure galleons on their way back from South America
• English Catholics, persecuted by Queen Elizabeth, had asked King Philip of Spain for help
• Mary Queen of Scots, before Elizabeth had her executed, had named King Philip as her heir
 Though only sixteen Spanish ships were sunk in battle, the Armada was forced to sail round the north of Scotland on the way back to Spain. More than sixty ships and nearly 20,000 men were lost in fierce storms. The battered remnants of the Armada finally reached Spain more than a year after their defeat at the hands of Drake and Admiral Howard.

We shared a bottle of sack* after the show. He asked me why I was in the country and what I was going to do next.

Grudgingly, I admitted that I hadn't a clue.

Then he gave a big grin and flung an arm round my shoulders. "There's no money in these provincial tours," he said. "I'm going back to London, where the action is. Stick with me, kid; we'll make a fortune."

Hmm, I thought, I quite fancy doing a bit of acting and could do with the money. I've also had enough of Pinky going on about his beastly water closet.

So it's back to the capital I go!

*A white wine from Spain.

Inky Shakespeare and I are getting very depressed. We've been in London now for over two months and we still haven't got any work.

We were drinking at the Boar's Head tavern last night and Shakespeare got all homesick and weepy. He showed me a miniature portrait of his wife.
"Anne Hathaway," he said.

I said I was sure she hath, but what was her name?

He said that *was* her name.

"Lovely," I said, praying silently that I'd never meet her late at night in a dark alley. If you ask me, the only reason Inky Shakespeare got into showbiz in the first place was so he'd have an excuse to get away from Stratford and Mrs Shakespeare. He was eighteen when he got married, she was twenty-six; a wedding at sword point* if ever I've heard of one.

*We would say a 'shotgun wedding' – Bacon is suggesting that Anne Hathaway may already have been expecting a child by William Shakespeare.

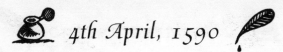

4th April, 1590

Blow my sackbut*! We've finally got a chance of work! We're auditioning for the Mr Big of the entertainment business – James Burbage. He started off as a carpenter, then in 1576 he built one of the first theatres. He's been putting on plays ever since, along with his two sons, Cuthbert and Richard.

Shakespeare told me the audition was at the Theatre.

What an imagination! James Burbage builds a theatre, and the most original thing he can think of to call it is the Theatre. He probably calls his cat the Cat.

* *An early form of trombone.*

🖋 7th April, 1590 🪶

As I sat waiting for my audition, I wondered who the Theatre's patron was. The Vagabond Laws say that all theatre companies must be sponsored. Usually the sponsor is some aristocratic twit who hopes that hanging about with actors will boost his popularity.

I asked Shakespeare who the company's patron was. He said, "He's Strange."

I said, "I daresay he's downright peculiar, but who is he?"

Shakespeare said that that's not what he meant. The patron of the Theatre was Ferdinando, Lord Strange, the son of the Earl of Derby.

We did our audition pieces. I gave a moving speech from *The Castle of Perseverance** and Shakespeare sang comic songs.

Shakespeare acquired a position as principal actor and I acquired a job holding horses.

* *A morality play first performed at Bury St Edmunds in 1425. It would have been very old hat in 1590.*

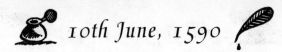

God's bodykins! What has Will Shakespeare got that I haven't?

I wrote down his background and mine to compare them, and see if I could work out why he gets all the plum jobs, while I end up standing all day up to my knees in horse-poo.

	William Shakespeare	Eggbert Noah Bacon
Born:	Stratford upon Avon, 23 April, 1564	London, 3rd July, 1565
Parents:	John Shakespeare, glover Mary Arden, gentlewoman	Sir Nicholas Bacon A certain gentlewoman
Brothers and Sisters:	Gilbert, Joan, Richard, Edmund	Francis (Half)
Wife:	Anne Hathaway	None
Children:	Susanna, born 1583 Hamnet and Judith (twins), born 1585	None (that I know of)
Schooling:	Dame Boggis' Petty School Stratford Grammar School	Stratford Grammar School Eton College Cambridge University
Qualifications:	Little Latin and less Greek	Double First in Classics and Philosophy
Previous Experience:	Trained as teacher, joined small theatre company: Patron, Sir Thomas Hesketh	Lying about doing nothing, as befits the son of a gentleman

I am more highly born, better educated, more handsome...
I simply don't understand it.

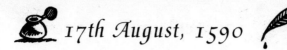

17th August, 1590

Curdle my crumhorn!* I've been promoted to Executive Vice-President in charge of advertising!

This means I have to go round sticking posters on walls:

Cominge Soone to the Theatre
(owner J Burbage Esq)

LORD STRANGE'S MEN

John Hemmings
Richard Burbage
William Kemp
George Bryan

Henry Condell
Augustine Phillips
Thomas Page
William Shakespeare

Richard (or Dickie, as he's known) Burbage gets all the meaty hero parts because his daddy owns the theatre. Phillips is the 'heavy' who plays all the baddies. Kemp is the clown, though if you ask me he's about as funny as toothache; for heaven's sake, this is 1590, you can't get laughs with a revolving ruff and baggy tights these days.

Not everybody's name is on the poster. There are three young lads; Alexander Cooke, Nicholas Tooley and Robert Gough, who play all the women's parts as girls aren't allowed to be on stage. I'm not sure they'll last the season. Cooke's voice is breaking, and as for Gough... well, you could see him as a beautiful young woman, if you happen to know lots of beautiful young women who need a shave.

* A wind instrument.

2nd September, 1590

Dickie Burbage is a ghastly little oik; he calls everyone "luvvie" or "darling". He also keeps going on about "Bums on seats, laddie, bums on seats", whatever that's supposed to mean. He's been moaning on for weeks about somebody called Christopher Marlowe, whose plays are packing them in at the Rose.

So Will Shakespeare and I went across the river to see what our rivals at the Rose theatre were up to.

Come to the Theatre
in Shoreditch

The greatest theatre
in London

prop: James Burbage

Company:

Lord Strange's Men

Come to the Rose
at Bankside

The finest theatre in
the Capital

Prop: Philip Henslowe
Principal Actor:
Edward Alleyn

— Company —

The Admiral's Men

They certainly know how to do things in style at the Rose. They've even got their own private barge to cross the River Thames, so you don't have to rub shoulders with smelly poor people. At the theatre these people are known as the groundlings because they stand on the floor in front of the stage. They don't pay as much, but when it rains, they get wet. The groundlings who come to the Theatre don't like the groundlings who go to the Rose. They go round in gangs chanting:

"We hate the Rose, we hate the Rose,
We are the Rose... HATERS!"

When the play started, I realised that some of the audience were sitting on benches at the side of the stage. I asked Shakespeare about this, and he said that they were rich kids who'd paid extra. They kept making remarks and trying to trip up the actors with their swords.

As if that wasn't enough, there were the nutcrackers: The actors could barely make themselves heard over the noise of people shouting to each other and cracking nuts.

None of this really mattered though because the play was absolutely terrible! It was supposed to be about Ancient Rome, but all the actors were wearing their normal clothes. There was no one who could act either; all the players just stood there waving their arms about and shouting.

The play was supposed to be a tragedy. But if you ask me, the only tragedy was that I paid tuppence to go in and see it!

24th September, 1590

Shakespeare has dropped himself right in it. Ever since we saw the play at the Rose, he's been going round saying what rubbish it was. He's also been boasting that he could write a better play with his quill in a sling. Eventually Dickie Burbage had enough, and told Shakespeare that if he was that good, he'd better write a play for the Theatre, and be quick about it!

Now Inky Shakespeare could always talk the hind legs off a cart horse, but he can't spell for toffee, or string a sentence together to save his life. He hardly even learnt to hold a pen, which is how he got his nickname. I can't wait to see how he's going to get out of this one.

3rd October, 1590

Shakespeare has come up with a perfect way to solve his problem (he thinks). He says he'll come up with the ideas for plays, and the characters and big speeches, and I can write them down and fill in the rest. When I've written the play, he'll sign his name to it and give it to Burbage.

I said he must be mad. He said didn't I think I could do it? I said of course I could do it, I've got a degree in Classics and Philosophy, but we'd never get away with it...

"Fair enough," he said, "spend the rest of your life putting up posters..."

So I bought a book called *Teach Yourself How to Wryte a Scripte.* It looks easy enough:

Chaptere One

1 – Thynk of a storie, and explayne it to the owner of a playhowse.

2 – If he thynkes it's a goode idea, wryte out the plotte.

3 – If the playhowse accepts the plotte, you wille get payed aboute £2 to wryte the scripte.

4 – Othere wryters can helpe. Some wryters wryte five or sixe playes at the same time. If the playe has five actes, a different wryter can work on each acte. (On the othere hand, the more wryters you use, the lesse monie you gette as you have to share it betweene all the wryters).

5 – Showe the scripte to the Master of the Revels, who will cut out all the naughty bits.

6 – If the scripte is accepted, you get payed aboute £4 or £5. The scripte now belonges to the companie.

I told Shakespeare that I may as well write the whole script myself, that way we'll only have to split the money two ways.

27th April, 1591

The play took me ages to write – and it didn't go down as well as we'd hoped. We had decided to write a revenge tragedy – that's the sort of play where the actors go round in cloaks hissing "Curses, foiled again" and there are lots of juicy murders.

It's all about a Roman called Titus Andronicus. I thought it had everything:

Titus kills one of his own sons in the first scene.

Titus's daughter has her tongue cut out and her hands chopped off.

The Emperor kidnaps two more of Titus' sons, and threatens to send Titus their heads unless he chops off his own hand and sends it to the Emperor.

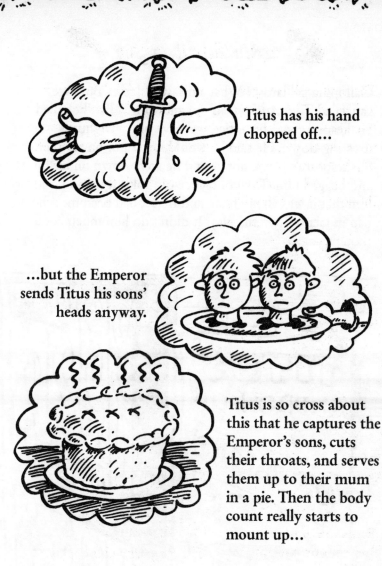

Titus has his hand chopped off…

…but the Emperor sends Titus his sons' heads anyway.

Titus is so cross about this that he captures the Emperor's sons, cuts their throats, and serves them up to their mum in a pie. Then the body count really starts to mount up…

Unfortunately, instead of gasping with horror, the audience fell about laughing and shouting 'funny' comments like "Don't eat the pies, missus!" and "He's inside you!"

28th April, 1591

Galloping galliards*! What a disaster! James Burbage cancelled *Titus Andronicus* this morning. Then he called Shakespeare into his office and gave him a frightful dressing-down. He said he would never put on another of Shakespeare's plays, not even if he went down on his knees and begged him. Then of course old Inky went and told him that it was all *my* fault, and that it had been me who had in fact written the play. It didn't do him much good though.

*A popular dance.

Well, Burbage doesn't own the only playhouse in London. We'll just have to sell our next play to Henslowe at the Rose. Shakespeare says it's no good copying bad, old-fashioned plays from classical times. If we're going to be successful, we're going to have to invent a whole new style of play.

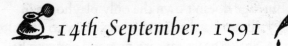

I finished the new play for Henslowe this morning and showed it to Will:

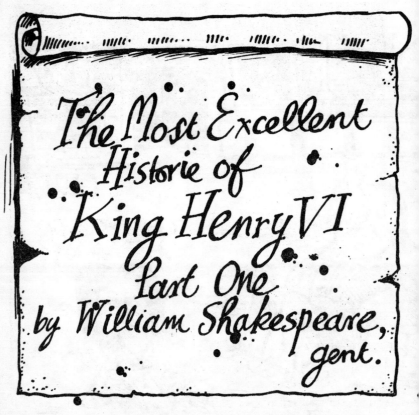

The Most Excellent Historie of King Henry VI Part One by William Shakespeare, gent.

I said it was all about the Wars of the Roses. He said never mind what it was about, did it have lots of the three 'P's?

I asked him coldly what the three 'P's might be.

He gave a grin. "What any play needs to be a success," he said. "Passion, Politics and Punch-ups."

I ask you! What a philistine!

Our new play is a terrific success! All the critics are raving about it!

YE STAGE

1st October 1591 *25 groats* Ye papere for ye luvvies

SWEET SMELLE OF SUCCESSE!

By our Drama Critic, Seymour Rubbish

And what about me?

Newcomer, Will Shakespeare, has written a real winner with Henry VI: Part One. The play, which tells how the Wars of the Roses began between the Royal Houses of Lancaster and York, has been playing to packed houses at the Rose. There's no doubt that this one will run and run!

AWARDS
The new play is already being tipped to sweep the board at next month's DAFTA awards.

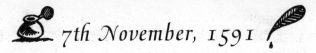

7th November, 1591

Will Shakespeare and I attended the DAFTA* awards last night. Anybody who's anybody in the theatre world was there. It was quite fun, with everyone being as nice as pie to each others' faces, and making sarcastic remarks behind each other's backs.

Richard "Dickie" Burbage

Edward Alleyn – Dickie Burbage's great rival at the Rose

* Daring and Funny Theatre Awards.

Shakespeare collected his award (or rather *our* award) and gave a speech in which he burst into tears and said he couldn't have done it without the help of all the 'little people' (that means me, I suppose).

Will Shakespeare

Ben Johnson - new kid on the block.

Christopher "Kit" Marlowe - brat-pack playwright

4th December, 1591

Henry VI: Part One has been doing excellent business for the Rose and James Burbage is furious! He said how dare we write plays for his rival Henslowe! Why hadn't we shown the play to him first? (Shakespeare tried to remind Burbage that he'd said he would never put on another play of ours after *Titus Andronicus*, but of course he wasn't listening.)

Burbage said if we wanted to stay with his company, we'd have to sign a contract:

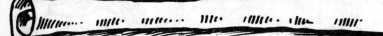

This AGREEMENT is made on the 4th daye
of Decembere, 1592

Between Eggbert Noah Bacon, gent. and William Shakespeare, gent. and the players of the Theatre, prop. James Burbage.

Ytem 1 – The Playwrights shall wryte only for James Burbage

Ytem 2 – The Playwrights shall wryte at least three plays every yeare

Ytem 3 – They shall wryte prologues and epilogues as required

Ytem 4 – They shall wryte new scenes for olde plays if asked

Ytem 5 – They shall add songes as required

Ytem 6 – They shall notte allowe their playes to be published

It all sounds a bit strict to me, but Will Shakespeare says if we don't sign it we won't get paid. Since I can't go back to Daddy, I'd better get on with it.

8th December, 1591

James Burbage insists that Shakespeare must write a sequel to *Henry VI: Part One* for the Theatre, so I went round to Inky's rat-infested lodgings in Shoreditch today to talk about it.

Shoreditch is an awful inner-city dump – narrow alleyways full of run-down tenements, alehouses, stables, dicing houses*, bowling alleys, and all those things poor people do to make their pathetic lives seem more bearable. The only thing to be said for it is that it's quite close to London Bridge, which is the only way to cross the river unless you fancy getting splashed with filthy river water by some clumsy oaf of a ferryman.

* Gambling dens where men would bet on the fall of dice.

And Shoreditch is so crowded!

There are over 200,000 people living in London. Of course, a lot of them don't live very long. Out of every ten people born:

- three die before their first birthday

- two more peg out by the age of five

- and two more before they reach fifteen

In other words, seven out of every ten people die before their fifteenth birthday. If I've survived this long, there's a fair chance I might live long enough to die an old, old man – at forty, say.

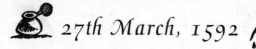

27th March, 1592

James Burbage reckons the new King Henry play will bring the crowds back from the Rose to his theatre. Actually, I've written Part III as well as Part II, just in case!

The posters are already up!

The Most Excellent Historie of

King Henry VI: Part Two

The Revenge
by William Shakespeare, gent.

The Most Excellent Historie of

King Henry VI: Part Three

This tyme, it's personal!
by William Shakespeare, gent.

13th May, 1592

Hang my hose out to dry! At long last, I've been paid!

All the money that people pay to see the plays is kept in a big box, and at the end of a season of plays the money in the 'box office' is divided up. The money from the seats in the galleries goes to the owners; the rest of the actors get the money the groundlings pay to stand in the yard.

Shakespeare collected the money he was due as the 'writer' of the *Henry VI* plays.

"Tell you what," he said, "we'll split it fifty-fifty."

I said that wasn't fair. I'd done all the hard work, it ought to be at least sixty-forty.

He thought for a bit, then said, "Have it your way," and gave me forty per cent of the money.

I'm still trying to work out how that happened.

17th June, 1592

Nudge my nakers*! Shakespeare shoved a roll of paper under my nose this morning and said, "You're on."

Apparently George Bryan, one of the actors, has come down with a spot of the plague, so I have to go on instead. We're doing *Henry VI: Part Three*.

"Here's your part," he said.

I looked at the roll of paper and asked him why I didn't get a proper book? He rolled his eyes and told me that there was only one copy of the whole play. The company scribe had made a copy of our script, and this had been chopped up to make a 'part' for each actor. Each part was then pasted together into a long roll, so each actor had his own lines but nobody else's. Shakespeare said there were two reasons for this:

1 – it was cheaper than copying out the whole book many times.
2 – it made it harder for a rival theatre to steal the script.

Some actors were bribed to let another company see their scripts, but if they only had their own lines, this wasn't much use. Shakespeare said some companies hired spies to go and watch performances at rival theatres, and write down as many lines as they could remember. He said plays weren't published as books, otherwise anybody would be able to put on any play without paying the writer, and then where would we be?

Where indeed?

* An early form of kettle drum.

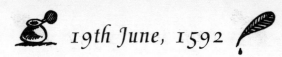

19th June, 1592

Gadzooks! Acting in this play is costing me a fortune!

I thought I'd just be able to go into the tiring house*
and pick up a spare costume, but Shakespeare explained to
me that all actors owned their own costumes, and wore
them no matter what part they were playing. The leading
actors had very expensive and elaborate costumes. They
also had to keep up with the latest fashion; an actor who
came on stage in last year's gear would be booed off.

So I've had to go out and buy some new clothes.

*Actors' changing room.

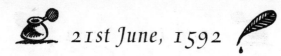

21st June, 1592

We are performing the play tomorrow night and I've only one more day to rehearse.

When I looked around during rehearsals today, I could see that everyone had a bigger scroll than me: in other words everyone else's part is bigger than mine! I also realised that some of the actors were playing two or three parts – they'd nip off and change their cloak, or hat, or wig or something and come back on pretending to be somebody else!

When we got to my first speech, I wasn't sure how to read it. I asked Shakespeare, "What's my motivation for this line?"

He snapped back, "Five shillings a week and bed and breakfast at the Boar's Head."

Well, excuuuuuuuuse me!

22nd June, 1592

Saved by the boil*! I was waiting to go on, scared half to death, when a messenger turned up and declared that he had been ordered to close down all the theatres because of the plague.

The order had come from the Burghers** of London. Shakespeare says they're a bunch of silly Burghers!

The theatres are closed until the end of September, so we're applying for a licence to perform outside London and then, hey nonny no, we're off on tour.

* One of the earliest symptoms of the plague was the appearance of boils, or buboes, in the groin and armpit of the victim.
** Members of the ruling council of London.

THE BLACK DEATH

Do you know a person who is...

- shivering
- aching all over

- suffering from splitting headaches

- developing black swellings in the groin and armpit?

Beware! That person has the PLAGUE!
Don't panic. Here's what to do:

- Draw a red circle on a piece of card, write the words 'Lord Have Mercy On Us' on it, and put it in the window to warn other people

- Do not go anywhere near the infected person

- Do not let anyone leave the house for twenty days

- Throw those who die into the plague-pit

WARNING FROM HM GOVERNMENT:
BUBONIC PLAGUE
CAN SERIOUSLY DAMAGE YOUR HEALTH.

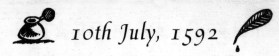

10th July, 1592

Bolts and shackles! Given a choice between touring and London, I think I'd rather head back to London and risk catching the plague.

We've been up, down and round the country playing at fairs, inns and anywhere that'll take us. People aren't always pleased to see us because they think we'll bring disease and cause riots – the cheek of it!

LORD STRANGE'S COMPANY PLAGUE TOUR

The Duke of Marlborough (OXFORD)

The Earl of Oxford (Marlborough)

Izzy Inn (Bath)

Gettem Inn (Bristol)

We're hardly making any money as there are plenty of other wandering players, acrobats, tumblers, dancers and clowns all trying to make a living.

And the travelling! The roads are either wet and muddy or dry and dusty. My poor feet are blistered and swollen from all the walking we've done. Only the main actors get to ride on the horses or in the wagon. The rest of us are called 'roadies'. I moaned at Will Shakespeare and asked why *I* had to walk. He said something about having to suffer for my art.

Odd socks! Who's the one doing all the work and who's the one getting all the credit?

I'm suffering for *his* art!

17th September, 1592

Ferdinando, our patron – now called the Earl of Derby since his father passed away – is in a spot of trouble with the Queen of England. The problem is, old Queen Liz hasn't got any kids (well, she never got married so it's hardly surprising). This means that no one knows who's going to be King or Queen when she kicks the royal bucket, so everybody is scheming away like mad and the court has more plots in it than a king-sized allotment.

Every so often, the Queen gets it into her head that someone's plotting against her (she's usually right) and this time the finger of suspicion had fallen on Ferdie.

Your Country doesn't need you

To help prove his innocence, he said he wanted Shakespeare to write a play which showed his family, the Stanleys, as jolly good eggs and supporters of the Crown.

Shakespeare said he'd think about it. By which he meant, of course, that *I* would think about it.

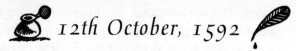

12th October, 1592

Shakespeare came round today and said, "How's it going, Streaky?"

I wish he wouldn't be so familiar.

I said it was 'going' quite well. I was writing a play for Ferdinando about Richard III.

Bad King Richard III, who was a Plantaganet... was winning the Battle of Bosworth against Henry Tudor...

until the Stanley family changed sides at the last minute... so Richard ended up with his head on a pole and Henry became King Henry VII (Queen Elizabeth's grandad).

Shakespeare didn't see how that would help Ferdinando, since it would remind the Queen that one of his ancestors was a traitor who'd changed sides. I said he was missing the point: Stanley had changed to the Tudor side, and since Queen Elizabeth was a Tudor, he'd chosen the *right* side.

I showed Shakespeare a few lines I'd written for the battle scene...

Shakespeare said it was a pathetic joke and anyway, it was supposed to be a serious scene. I said I was just trying to lighten the atmosphere a bit.

He said, "Why don't you have Richard cry:

Well, I suppose it has a certain ring to it, but I like my line better. Anyway, it won't be performed until the theatres open again (unless the Queen orders a performance at court).

30th October, 1592

Flush my waterworks! I was visiting Pinky Hartington again, and who should turn up? Only her Royal Majesty, Queen Elizabeth! It seems she'd heard about that disgusting water closet invention of Pinky's (he's calling it Ajax; I mean, *why*?) and decided to come and see how good it was.

I think she must have liked it, because she was on the throne all morning and when she came out, she said, "Most refreshing, good Master Hartington," and ordered one for her palace at Greenwich.

She was so pleased she invited Pinky to go to court for the Ascension Day jousts in November. She asked me to ask that nice Mr Shakespeare to put on a play for her at Christmas. I suggested *Richard III*, but she sniffed and said, "One is fed up with plays about one's family. One would like to see a nice comedy."

More work!

We performed our new comedy at court today.
Shakespeare insisted on calling it *The Taming of the
Shrew*... I was scared stiff that the Queen might be
offended by the play – it's about a woman being forced to
give in to her husband. However, since the Queen doesn't
have a husband, she obviously thought it didn't apply to
her, and laughed her head off (instead of chopping our
heads off).

So, it's another triumph! What's more, I'm really
enjoying living it up at court!

CHRISTMAS MENU

STARTERS:
Capon broth
Pike with sauce
Stewed Carp

MAIN COURSE: Roast Oxen
Boar's head
Roast Goose
Roast Beef and Mustard
Lamb stuffed with garlic
Capon boiled with leeks
Shoulder of Veal
Roast Chicken
Peacock pie
Venison pasty

DESERT:
Roasted Pears
Apples
Cold Tarts
Marzipan and sugar Castles
Cake
Cheese

DRINK:
Sack: a crisp white wine from Spain
Burgundy: a full-bodied red wine
                    from France
Canary: a fresh young wine from the
                    Canary Islands
Strong Ale: try one of our Guest Beers;
'Huff-cap' 'Angel's Food' 'Dragon's Milk'

4th January, 1593

Nobody did any work over the twelve days of Christmas, but there was much splendid music. Sometimes the Queen would play for us on the virginals*.

Then there was dancing, and mumming plays**.

The whole thing finished with the most amazing party. The servants chose a Lord of Misrule, and off they went to church in a procession (they call it "Lusty Guts") banging drums, tootling pipes and ringing bells fit to wake the dead.

* An early form of harpsichord.
** Short traditional plays, usually about St George.

When the servants came back, all we gentry had to serve them dinner, as if we were the servants and they were the masters. It was rather fun for a day but it would be ghastly if it were that way round all the time!

The Lord of Misrule let the servants do anything they liked, but most of them were fairly well behaved, knowing that next morning, we'd be in charge again.

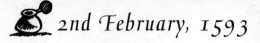 # 2nd February, 1593

The theatres are still closed because of the plague in London.

Hundreds of dogs have been killed. It is thought that they carry the plague, so if anyone gets hold of a stray then it's chop chop, and off to doggy heaven*.

Mind you, some of the radical religious Puritan nutters reckon that the plague is caused by something very different!

> The cause of plagues is sin, if you look to it well: and the cause of sin is plays; therefore the cause of plagues is plays.

Some people!

* Elizabethans didn't realise that the bubonic plague was carried by fleas.

3rd March, 1593

Burst my buboes*! I felt terrible yesterday so I dragged myself out to see the local doctor, just to make sure I hadn't caught the big P and wasn't about to join the celestial choirs.

The doctor asked me if I was a private patient. When I said I wasn't, he told me he'd put me on the waiting list. In the meantime I should drink a pint of hedgehog wee and come back in six months, unless of course I was already dead. He also gave me some leaflets...

* Plague sores.

← Ye head

Ye chest →

Ye thingy

← Ye knee

GET WELL

For sample

BURPA

Looking after you, because you deserve it.

The human body contains four humours:

blood
phlegm*
choler**
melancholy***

leech

When a person is well, the humours are in balance, but living at today's hectic pace of life means that this balance can easily become upset. If you have too much of any one humour, you will get sick.

SUFFERING FROM PLAGUE?

- Put rue**** on your window sill
- Put rosemary in your ears and nose
- If you get any plague sores, kill a pigeon and put it on the sores!

* This humour causes calmness.
** Excess of this causes anger.
*** Sadness.
**** A herb.

Let **BURPA** help you with all your other ailments

ENROL TODAY

TOP BURPA TREATMENTS:

- Suffering from an excess of blood! Try a leech treatment! Let us put a dozen carefully chosen leeches on your body and they will suck your blood out!
- Suffering from a bad liver? Simply drink a mouthful of ale mixed with nine lice every morning for a week
- Are your feet swollen? Boil up a red-haired dog in oil. Mix this with worms, pigs marrow and herbs and smear over your foot.

SPECIAL OFFER TODAY

OTHER TOP REMEDIES INCLUDE:

- Powdered human skull
- Scrapings from the skull of an executed criminal
- Mixture of cream and cat's blood

Hmm, I thought. I'm feeling better already...

16th March, 1593

William Shakespeare is now a major showbiz celebrity. He's even started to smoke big cigars and call everyone "Sweetheart". It seems strange that no one has yet strangled him for doing this.

Perhaps all this success going *to* his head explains why all the hair is going *from* his head! He's getting as bald as a cannon ball.

While I've been writing plays, Shakespeare's been busy writing poetry! He's written a long poem called *Venus and Adonis*, which he's dedicated to the Earl of Southampton. He only did it to flatter the Earl, win his support and get money out of him – and it worked! Mind you, he'd have got a better sponsorship deal if he'd called it *Vimto and Adidas*.

30th April, 1594

There haven't been any reports of plague this spring, so the theatres are back in business. James and Dickie Burbage have agreed to join forces with Philip Henslowe and Edward Alleyn from the Rose this year, to cut costs. They've asked us to write a new play. I've started one about a couple of young lovers from Cheapside whose families don't get on, so they run away to get married. I want to call it *Ronnie and Josephine*.

By the way, the Theatre's patron, Ferdinando, Earl of Derby, died recently in mysterious circumstances. Well, not that mysterious; people do tend to die when you poison them with arsenic. But it means that James Burbage will have to find a new patron.

[

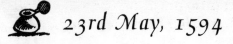

23rd May, 1594

James Burbage has found a new patron: Henry Carey, the Lord Chamberlain (the Queen's top fixer). So now the company will be called "The Lord Chamberlain's Men".

Will Shakespeare doesn't like my ideas for *Ronnie and Josephine*. According to him, we ought to:

- change the setting to Verona in Italy (because it's more exotic, he says)
- make the families two noble houses who've been quarrelling for years
- have the young lovers die at the end because it's "more romantic".

I took some notes while he ranted on:

I mean, what a load of drivel! And he wants to call the young lovers Romeo and Juliet. He's made me change some lines as well.

But I wanted Josephine to say, "Ronnie's a stupid name".

Oh, Romeo, Romeo, wherefore art thou Romeo?

Honestly! It's going to be a disaster, I just know it!

31st May 1594 *25 groats*   *Ye papere for ye luvvies*

ONE IN THE EYE FOR MARLOWE!

Playwright Christopher Marlowe was murdered in a pub brawl yesterday. He was having a meal with playboy chums Ingram Frizer, Nicholas Skeres and Robert Poley when a row broke out over the bill and Frizer stabbed Marlowe in the eye.

Petite, vivacious barmaid Eleanor Bull (28) said: "He seemed like a really nice young man."

CONSPIRACY?

Sources close to the Government revealed exclusively to *Ye Stage* that Marlowe was under investigation by the Secret Service over allegations that he was a closet Catholic.

The Secret Service has had it in for Marlowe ever since they threw poor old Tommy Kyd* in prison for writing pro-Catholic pamphlets, and he tried to save himself by telling them that Marlowe had written them. Frizer works for Thomas Walsingham, who's one of the Queen's top spymasters; and Skeres works for the Earl of Essex. It's anybody's guess who Marlowe worked for, probably both of them at the same time. Anyway, it looks to me as if one of them put a contract out on him.

Will Shakespeare is trying to pretend that he's really upset about Marlowe, but Marlowe was the only serious competition around and I can tell he's secretly thrilled to know his arch-rival is out of the way. In fact, come to think of it, I swear I saw him chatting away to Frizer at the Bull's Head only a couple of weeks ago.

I wonder…

Thomas Kyd was a playwright best known for The Spanish Tragedy. *He died in prison the year following Marlowe's death.*

Well, I'd never have believed it, but *Romeo and Juliet* is a smash hit! People are queuing in the rain for days before each performance, just to make sure they can get in to see it! The souvenir shop has run out of "I Love Romeo" T-shirts and locks of Juliet's hair (as Juliet is played by a boy, they're buying bits of an old horse-hair wig, but as long as they're happy…)

The play is making so much money that Burbage has decided to part company with Henslowe again. So Henslowe and his Admiral's Company are staying on at the Rose, and we're moving back to our old playhouse, the Theatre.

Will Shakespeare is going to be a shareholder with the new company. This means he'll get a bigger slice of the profits, so he's taken to smoking even bigger cigars. What a show-off!

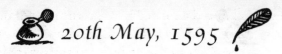

20th May, 1595

We only managed to get in a few performances of our new play, *Richard II*, before all the theatres closed again because of riots. This time people are rioting because of bread; there's not enough of it, and it's too expensive.

Funnily enough, you can buy almost anything in London except bread. Going shopping is a messy business – even if

you don't fall into the open drain that runs down the middle of every street, or get trodden on by cattle on their way to market, you can hardly move in the streets for carts. There are workshops on either side of the street and the noise is terrible, but the smell is even worse! Shopkeepers stand in every doorway shouting: "What do ye lack?" Street vendors try to sell you everything from pies to mouse traps, and pickpockets and cutpurses* try to steal your money before you have the chance to spend it.

* Men wore their purses hanging off their belts: a cutpurse would cut off their purses with a sharp knife.
** Cucumbers

The streets are always full of life. There are running battles between gangs of boys from rival schools and, as if that isn't enough, there are always parties of sailors or tourists from France, Germany or Holland standing around gawping.

The best time to go shopping is in the early morning before it gets crowded. The open-air markets get going at about five a.m.

The shops open at about six a.m. They don't have names over their doors because servants do most of the shopping and servants can't read. Instead, the shops have brightly painted signs with pictures of roses and dragons and lions and things so that you can tell your servant to buy such-and-such a thing "at the sign of the green dragon". It's easy enough to find what you want; if you need a chicken, you go to a street called The Poultry; if you need some nails, you can get them in Ironmongers' Lane, and you can buy leather goods in Skinners' Lane.

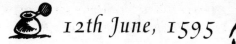

12th June, 1595

The playhouses have been allowed to open again; there's even a new one!

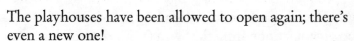

Bring the family to the **Swan**

London's brand new playhouse is opening soon on Bankside, near the Rose.

The **Swan** has...

- top class entertainment
- first rate facilities including hospitality suites
- parking for 20 carriages and 100 horses
- flint walls for safety
- seating for 3,000 people
- marble pillars!

Marble - hah! Painted — wood me thinks

3rd July, 1595

We've heard that Henslowe from the Rose is worried about competition from the Swan (as it's right on his doorstep), so he's gone to town on the special effects: he's had a new contraption fitted in his theatre so that he can have the gods coming down from heaven on golden thrones.

All a bit pathetic if you ask me, just relying on trickery when you're short of ideas; but Will Shakespeare is beside himself with jealousy. I daresay we'll have one of these silly contraptions at the Theatre before long.

17th July, 1595

Will Shakespeare and I have another smash hit on our hands! *A Midsummer Night's Dream* is packing them in. Well, people love a good panto. Will Kemp, our company joker, is complaining like mad because he's playing Bottom, the weaver, and he has to wear a fake donkey's head for most of the play. He says it's hot in there and it itches.

The Theatre Presentes

Thereare fayries in the garden
....at our Bottom!

A Midsummer Nights Dream
by William Shakespeare

now showing

Top play!

Played by The Lord Chamberlains Men.

I've got a bit part in the play, too. I play Snout and I have to pretend to be a wall. I overheard Will Shakespeare make some crude and unfunny remark about the part being just right for someone of my acting ability.

The man has no appreciation of my talent!

James Burbage has plans for another theatre, in the Blackfriars. This building used to be a monastery, then it became a hall where choirboys performed their plays.

The trouble with the Theatre and the Rose is that they're open to the sky, and it can be freezing cold. The Blackfriars is indoors; it doesn't hold nearly as many people as the Theatre, but it's a lot more comfortable. It's all-weather and all-seater.

Whenever anyone mentions the new theatre, Will Shakespeare goes all misty-eyed and says you can't watch plays properly unless you're standing, and that the atmosphere just isn't the same, moan moan moan... Rubbish! Give me a nice comfortable seat any day.

I'm pleased to say that the Blackfriars is in a very up-market area, but the people who come to our plays are a rougher lot than the gentlefolk residents. I hope the admission prices will keep the rabble out, but some of the locals don't seem too happy about it already.

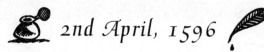

Will Shakespeare and I have been discussing the new play I'm writing, *The Merchant of Venice*. We've pinched the plot from some Italian stories.

The Theatre Presentes

Shylock bankrolled his friend
Now he wants his cut....

The Merchant of — Venice —

by William Shakespeare

smash hit!

It's so cool!

Played by The Lord Chamberlain's Men

"Don't Go Taking My Heart!"

Antonio (the Merchant) has signed a piece of paper to say Shylock (the moneylender) can cut out his heart if he doesn't pay up (the fool!). Portia is the judge in the case, and I wanted her to say: "Fair enough, but don't get blood all over the floor."

But Will Shakespeare's changed this to:

The quality of mercy is not strain'd; It droppeth as the gentle rain from heaven upon the place beneath...

And she goes on like this until she finds a legal loophole and gets Antonio off with a caution.

Oh yes, very fine, I'll grant you. Very poetic, but where's the *drama*?

13th August, 1596

Poor old Will Shakespeare. His only son, Hamnet, died a couple of days ago. He was only eleven.

Shakespeare just heard today. He's dreadfully cut-up about it. He's still got two daughters; Susanna and Judith (Hamnet's twin sister), but he doesn't see much of them. He didn't see much of his son either, come to that; the kids live with their mother in Stratford and Shakespeare only goes back there in Lent when the London playhouses are closed.

17th October, 1596

Zounds and Lord 'a' mercy! I was lucky to escape with my life this evening! On the way home from work, I was set upon by a gang of thieves. They took all my money, and most of my clothes! The Watch* made me look over some mug shots to try and identify the men who'd attacked me.

Ralph the Ruffler: top thief wanted for burglary and GBH**

Pete the Prigger of Pransers: wanted for TWOC*** two horses

Catpurse Charlie: wanted for theft and pickpocketing

Highwayman Harry: holds people up on roads and robs them

Dummerer Des: beggar, pretends to be dumb

Katie the kinchin Mort: lures men up dark alleys to be robbed

Whipjack Willie: beggar, pretends to be a retired sailor

Moon man Mike: asks permission to sleep in barns then steals chickens

* The Tudor Police.
** Grievous Bodily Harm.
*** Taking Without Owner's Consent.

20th October, 1596

Beat my tabor*! Will Shakespeare's father, John, has been given his own coat of arms. Only the top people get them; it seems that young William had a few words with the right people at court. It just goes to show how much influence Shakespeare's got now that he's a big success – all thanks to me! He's looking as pleased as a dog with two tails and smoking cigars it needs two strong men to lift.

NON SANZ DROICT

I notice that the Shakespeare coat of arms shows a falcon *shaking* a *spear*. How original, methinks – not! The motto means "Not Without Right", in case anybody's interested.

* A small hand drum.

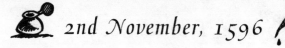

2nd November, 1596

Galloping goosepimples! We're not getting a warm indoor theatre after all! There's a petition to keep us out of the Blackfriars (just because the noise of hammering from carpenters getting it ready was keeping everybody awake at night). This is bad news, especially as the first signature on it is our own patron! There's going to be trouble! We can't stay in the Theatre for much longer, it's falling apart.

To her most gracious Majesty, Queen Elizabeth, we, the residents of Blackfriars, present this most humble Petition:

We, the undersigned, beg that you wille not allowe playes to be putte on at the Blackfriars Theatre, because this will cause much NOYSE and NUISANCE and attract the WRONG SORTE OF PERSONE

SIGNED:

Henry Carey, Lord Chamberlain
Hugo First, doorman
Turpin Soff, merchant
Les Tawders, innkeeper
Robin M Blind, lawyer
Mal Demerre, sailor
Justice Wunce, magistrate

Lloyd Blessus, Bishop of London
Pete Ziccato, musician
Walter Wall, carpet layer
Adam Shotoff, soldier (ret'd)
William Harry Mee, bachelor
Barry M Quick, undertaker
Billy O'Pork, butcher

2nd February, 1597

James Burbage, Dickie's father, died today. He'll never see his actors in the Blackfriars Theatre now, which is a pity.

Will Shakespeare has decided to go back to historical drama. He showed me a list of English Kings:

King
Richard II DONE
Henry IV
Henry V
Henry VI DONE (in three parts)
Edward VI DONE (in Henry VI)
Edward V Not worth doing
(he was king for about ten minutes)

Richard III DONE

The plan is to finish off all the Kings listed and write plays about Henry IV and Henry V. Then we'll have covered over one hundred years of English history! Or rather he'll have covered it and *I'll* have written it!!

YE STAGE

24th April 1597 *25 groats* *Ye papere for ye luvvies*

'ONE WAS AMUSED!'

**By our Drama Critic,
Seymour Rubbish**

England's leading playwright, Will Shakespeare, scored another phenomenal success yesterday with his new smash hit, **The Merry Wives of Windsor**. Rumour has it that Shakespeare wrote the play in just TWO WEEKS at the command of her Majesty, Queen Elizabeth. **TOP BANANA!** This latest success is expected to

deliver a box-office bonanza for the ever-popular West Midlands whizz-kid, and confirm his position as Number One Draw with royalty and commoner alike.

He didn't, I did. and does my hand ache!

Will Shakespeare has a lot of top-notch friends at court these days. He's very pally with the Earl of Essex. I'm not sure this is a good idea – Essex is a bit of a hothead, and I'll be surprised if he stays out of trouble for long.

"What do you think of this?" Will Shakespeare asked me as we were sitting in the Red Lion quaffing a few quarts of ale. He shoved a piece of paper under my nose.

FOR SALE

New Place, Stratford
The second biggest house in Stratford!
Highly desirable family home
Located on the corner of Chapel Street and Chapel Lane, Stratford-upon-Avon
Originally built in around 1500, this fine brick and timber building needs some renovation work.
Sixty ft wide, Seventy ft deep!
Ten fireplaces with full WFCH (Wood Fired Central Heating)
Complete with two gardens, two orchards and two barns
PRICE £60 in silver
Contact William Underhill of Stratford

"Very nice," I said. "Thinking of buying it?"

"I've bought it," he replied. "It's something for the wife and kids to live in. I feel a bit guilty about not seeing them much."

That's right, I thought to myself, keep them happy and keep them out of the way, while you stay in London living it up!

"So, we'd better start writing a few more plays to pay for it," he said.

Hmm, I thought, you mean *I'd* better start writing a v more plays.

28th July, 1597

Will Shakespeare came in today with steam coming out of his ears: he told me all the theatres have been closed down *again*!

I asked him why, and he said, "Isle of Dogs!"

Well, I love dogs myself, but why should that close all the theatres?

He showed me the front page of the paper:

YE STAGE

28th July 1597   25 groats   Ye papere for ye luvvies

BEN BUSTED!

Playwright Ben Jonson is in prison tonight after being arrested during the first performance of his new play, *The Isle of Dogs*, at the Swan theatre. Jonson is the most popular playwright in London after Shakespeare, but he's been in trouble before for poking fun at the authorities.

THE SHOW WON'T GO ON!

All the theatres in London have been closed following Jonson's arrest. All the actors who took part in *The Isle of Dogs* have also been thrown into prison, and the Bankside magistrates are threatening to demolish the Swan.

Ye Stage says: **"If you don't like England, Ben, why don't you buzz off?"**

YOUR HOROSCOPE:
Unfortunately our Astrologer, Mystic Mildred, has been burnt for Witchcraft.

Will Shakespeare's pal, Ben Jonson, is in trouble – again!
He only got out of prison a few months ago, and he's
really done it this time!

Ben Jonson fought a duel with
George Spenser, an actor with Philip
Henslowe's company.

Spenser went down in the third...
and stayed down. A doctor
pronounced him dead.

Jonson could have been hanged for murder, but the
cunning little beast got off on a technicality. He was able
to claim protection under the old law of Benefit of
Clergy, which says anyone who can read and write gets
let off a first offence.

Jonson won't get off totally, though. He'll be branded
with the letter 'T' on his thumb; this stands for Tyburn,
the place where criminals are executed, and shows that
he's already had his chance and won't get away with any
more crimes!

23rd December, 1598

Well this is good news to get just before Christmas – NOT!

Apparently the lease has run out on the land the Theatre stands on, and the owner, Giles Alleyn, is refusing to renew it at reasonable terms; which means he can throw us out, and turn the Theatre into a supermarket or carpet warehouse or something.

So we can't remain at the Theatre and we're not allowed to go to the Blackfriars. This has put a drain on our company's finances, so Dickie Burbage has decided to sell some of our plays to publishers. They will print them as quartos* and sell them at sixpence a time. This means that we get some ready cash, but it also means that anyone who wants to can put the plays on without paying us anything.

Still, they're mostly old plays, and I can always write new ones.

Paperback books made from sheets of paper that had been folded into quarters.

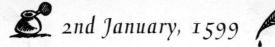

2nd January, 1599

Crease my codpiece! If I hadn't seen it with my own eyes, I'd never have believed it!

Dickie Burbage and Will Shakespeare went missing over Christmas. When they came back on Boxing Day they had with them a carpenter called Peter Street and a load of workmen (what they must have paid them for working over the Christmas holiday I shudder to think). They started to pull the Theatre apart, piece by piece. Then they transported the whole lot of it over the river, and rebuilt it practically next door to the Rose. And they did the whole thing in *six days*!

The new theatre is going to be called the Globe. Will Shakespeare says he wants it opened in May, and he wants a brand-new play for the first performance.

I'd give a few shillings to see Henslowe's face when he finds out that Shakespeare and Burbage have moved in next door, but I'd give a lot more to see the face of Giles Alleyn when he finds out that the whole Theatre has disappeared!

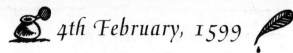

4th February, 1599

I saw the plans for the Globe. VERY impressive.
  Someone's going to make a lot of money out of this
venture. But you can be sure it won't be me*!

Thatched roof

Balcony

Galleries

Tiringhouse

Trapdoor

Stage

Yard

* The Burbages put up half the capital for the building of the Globe.
Heminges, Shakespeare, Phillips, Poe and Kemp found the rest of the
money. This meant Shakespeare owned ten per cent of the new playhouse.

THE GLOBE THEATRE
GALA OPENING!

Be there at the opening of the newest and the best theatre in London!
A new blockbuster by William Shakespeare

Henry V

When the going gets tough... the Toff gets going!

16 May at 2 p.m.

Ticket prices

Groundlings (standing only) - One penny
Lower gallery - Tuppence (cushions, a penny extra)
Upper gallery - Sixpence
On the stage - Sixpence
Gentlemans room /box - 1 shilling

HURRY! HURRY! HURRY!
— Only 2,500 tickets available —

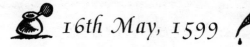

The Globe opened today with *Henry V*. What a triumph!
At two o'clock I raised the flag, which shows Hercules
carrying the world on his shoulders, and the play began.

The punters loved it; hardly surprising as it's all about
how the English stuffed the French at the Battle of
Agincourt. English audiences do like a play about the
French getting beaten.

The Globe is a real state-of-the-art theatre, even though
it's open air! It has a throne that comes down from the
heavens, just like Henslowe's. Will Shakespeare's been
playing with it for days. He couldn't find an excuse to
use it in *Henry V*, but I'm sure he'll think of something
later on.

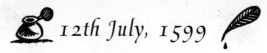

Curdle my codpiece: Will Kemp has left the company!

He had a huge argument with Will Shakespeare yesterday. He'd had a few beers too many and arrived drunk for the performance of *Henry V*. He managed to stagger his way through it, but he was fined ten shillings. It's all part of the contract he's got.

He came moaning to me, but I said he should have read the small print (mind you, I suspect that he has difficulty reading the large print!).

Contract of Employ

THE SMALL PRINT
I agree to pay the following fines

Being late for a rehearsal – twelve pence
Missing a rehearsal – two shillings
Not learning my part – three shillings
Being drunk on stage – ten shillings
Missing a performance – twenty shillings
Stealing costumes – forty pounds
Signed
Will Kemp

The Globe

He stormed out of the theatre and hasn't been seen since!

Still, it's no loss that Kemp's left the Globe – people don't want baggy-trousered comedians any more.

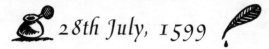

28th July, 1599

Darn my doublet! Will Shakespeare's aristocratic friend, the Earl of Essex, is in deep trouble today! I cut the article out of the paper:

YE STAGE

28th July 1599   25 groats   Ye papere for ye luvvies

ESSEX GRILLED!

The Earl of Essex, who was once the favourite of the Queen, is in disgrace today following his failed expedition to sort out the Irish rebellion. Instead of giving the rebel leader, Lord Tyrone, a good bashing, he signed a treaty with him.

HER MAJESTY IS NOT AMUSED.

The Queen was not interested in any excuses, and left Essex to cool his heels in prison.

The Queen is pretty old and crotchety these days, and I'll be surprised if Essex takes this lying down; he's very ambitious, better at fighting than thinking, and some people say he's got his eye on the throne when Elizabeth pegs out.

21st September, 1599

Griddle my girdle! When is Will Shakespeare going to stop interfering with my playwriting?

Today I was watching the first performance of *Julius Caesar*; but when it came to the bit where Mark Antony has a go at the crowd, my jaw dropped. The line I'd written for him to say was:

"I say you chaps! Hold on a second! Oh, do be quiet and listen!"

What Mark Antony *actually* said was:

Friends! Romans! Countrymen! Lend me your ears...

For heaven's sake, what's that supposed to mean? Does he want them to cut their ears off and throw them at him? I tackled Shakespeare after the show and he admitted that he'd changed the line because he thought his version was 'more poetic'. He didn't even bother to tell me!

Who does he think he is?!

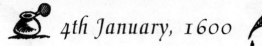

4th January, 1600

We're at Richmond Palace for New Year, putting on plays for the court. The Queen liked our new one, *Twelfth Night*. Quite frankly, I'm amazed she understood it!

The heroine, Viola, is a girl, played by a boy (because girls aren't allowed on stage), so we have a boy dressed as a girl. But then Viola pretends to be a boy, so we have a boy dressed up as a girl pretending to be a boy. Then Olivia (who's also played by a boy) starts to fancy Viola because he… or she… thinks he… or she… is a boy, when really she's a girl, but actually he's a boy…

Is it just me, or is this seriously weird?

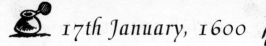 17th January, 1600

Well, ruffle my ruff! Anything you can do, we can do better! Philip Henslowe and Edward Alleyn from the Rose have decided to build a new playhouse because they're so jealous of the Globe's success. It's going to be on the opposite side of the River Thames in Cripplegate.

They've even employed Peter Street to build it and it appears that it's going to be practically a copy of the Globe*.

They're calling it the Fortune. Probably because that's what it'll cost to build**!

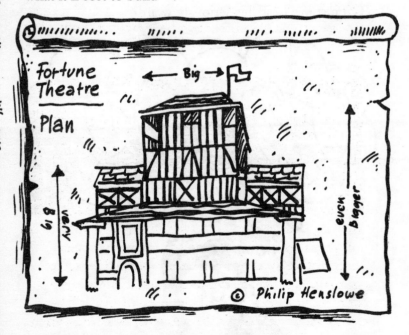

Fortune Theatre Plan

← Big →

very Big

even Bigger

© Philip Henslowe

* *The building was square, not a round 'O' like the Globe.*
** *Peter Street was paid £440 for his work (over a quarter of a million pounds in today's money). The total cost to Alleyn and Henslowe was around £1,320 (three quarters of a million pounds in today's money).*

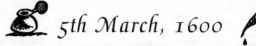 5th March, 1600

I am getting so sick of Will Shakespeare interfering with my lines.

I've been trying to write a new play called *Omlette, the Potty Prince of Poland*, but Shakespeare keeps changing things.

First he didn't like the title and changed it to *Hamlet*.

Then I wanted the hero to think about killing himself, so I wrote a wonderful soliloquy (that's when a character talks to himself; in real life it's called 'going mad', but in plays it's called a soliloquy):

"Shall I top myself, or not?

If I snuff it, I'll have nothing more to worry about…"

Of course, that wasn't good enough for Mr Shakespeare, so we ended up with:

Well, it's a damn silly question if you ask me. In fact, the whole play's pretty silly. By the end there are so many bodies on stage the actors can barely move. (He reckons you can't make a hamlet without breaking a few eggs.) I reckon this new play will be a complete turkey. It'll be lucky to last a week, particularly as we now have children putting on plays in the Blackfriars theatre and the audiences are flocking to see the little darlings.

The Globe Theatre Presentes

Wild and whacky goings on in daffy Denmark!
A crafty King, his nutty Nephew, a grisly Ghost —
and bodyes all over the playce!

HAMLET

by William Shakespeare

— PLAYED BY —

The Lord Chamberlain's
Men

10th March, 1600

I heard today that Will Kemp has just completed a sponsored dance! Apparently he jigged all the way from London to Norwich! He completed it in only nine days (although he had lots of rest in between the dancing days*).

The word is that he's qualified for the European Champion Morris Dancing League – he's going to dance all over Europe to Rome**.

If you ask me, the foreigners are welcome to him and his awful jokes.

* Kemp completed the dance on 8th March, 1600.
** Kemp danced all the way to Rome in 1601.

13th August, 1600

The Queen let the Earl of Essex out of prison today, and the first thing he did was to write to King James VI of Scotland saying that the Prime Minister, Lord Cecil, was an absolute beast for keeping him locked up so long. Not very tactful!

The census figures also came out today. I was astonished to find that the population of England and Ireland together is five and a half *million*! Can you imagine it? If it keeps on going up at this rate, we'll all be treading on each others' toes!

Christmas Day, 1600

Another working Christmas at court. Everyone else is busy playing silly games like *Hoodman Blind**, *Shove Ha'penny*, *Skittles* and all sorts of dice and card games. Will Shakespeare is limping because he got talked into playing *Dun is in the Mire*, a stupid game where you have to lift a heavy log of wood and drop it on each others' feet – serves him right.

* *Blind Man's Buff.*

While he's been fooling about, the rest of us have been rehearsing *As You Like It* so we can perform to the Queen on Boxing Day.

It's another mind-bending situation…

The heroine of *As You Like It* is Rosalind, who of course is a girl, even though the actor who's playing her is a boy. However, in the play, Rosalind runs away to the Forest of Arden and pretends to be a boy. So now he… or she… is a boy pretending to be a girl pretending to be a boy…

You could say that the play is about as confusing as the political state of the country. Nobody knows who's going to be King (or Queen) when Liz pops her clogs. The clever money is on King James of Scotland. A few of the hotheads at court may have their own ideas. The whole thing is giving me a headache!

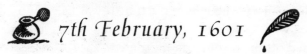

7th February, 1601

Fie on't! Passion, Politics and Punch-ups aren't just in plays! Methinks Will Shakespeare and I are in BIG trouble.

7th February 1601 25 groats Ye papere for ye luvvies

ESSEX GOES FOR BROKE!

The Earl of Essex was captured today after trying to lead a rebellion against her most gracious Majesty, Queen Elizabeth.

The excitable Earl hasn't been flavour of the month for a long time. Palace sources say that he has had a lot of rows with the Queen, who at one point boxed his ears.

REVOLTING BEHAVIOUR!

Earlier today, Essex tried to raise a rebellion against the Queen, but he and his few followers were captured. This follows last month's arrest of the Earl of Southampton, whose page had his hand cut off in the fighting.

Ye Stage says: "Hanging's too good for Essex!"

Southampton used to be Will Shakespeare's patron. What's more, the day before he tried to take over the Government, Essex made Will Shakespeare and Dickie Burbage perform *Richard II*. We hadn't performed it for ages and the actors couldn't remember the lines, but Essex wouldn't take no for an answer and even paid for the performance. I thought at the time it was fishy. Why did Essex want us to put on a play about a monarch being kicked off the throne and murdered?

Well, now we know why, and we're expecting to be dragged off to the Tower for an appointment with Mr Rack.

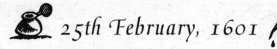

25th February, 1601

I think we've got away with it. Essex was executed today, but the Queen has decided to make Southampton's punishment life imprisonment, so things seem to be calming down.

The word from court is that Queen Elizabeth is still pretty miffed that we put on *Richard II*, so Will Shakespeare and the others are keeping their heads down until the row blows over.

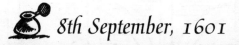

8th September, 1601

Another death. Will Shakespeare's father passed away. He died a "gentleman", so it means that his title will pass down to his son. Shakespeare's gone off to Stratford for the funeral, and I've pottered down to Pinky Hartington's for a few days to get away from London, which is a pretty depressing place at the moment.

Even before his father died, Shakespeare was getting incredibly gloomy. He kept saying we ought to write more serious plays, like *Hamlet*, where there are lots of murders and everybody dies at the end.

That's a pity because the play I'm working on at the moment is a comedy!

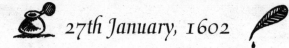

27th January, 1602

Batter my bum-roll!* The whole country is having the
jitters. Nobody knows when the Queen will die, and
nobody knows what will happen when she does.
Everyone's afraid of another Spanish invasion, or someone
like Essex leading another revolt.

I've finished the new comedy and called it *All's Well
That Ends Well*. Will Shakespeare just looked at the title
and said, "Let's hope so." Then he went on biting his nails.

* *Padding used in Elizabethan dresses.*

YE STAGE

24th March 1603   25 groats   Ye papere for ye luvvies

SO LONG MA'AM

In the early hours of today, Queen Elizabeth passed away at Richmond Palace, ending her long reign.

The Archbishop of Canterbury spent last night praying with her. He says she died "mildly, like a lamb; easily, like a ripe apple from the tree."

The official announcement of her death came at ten o'clock this morning and was made by Robert Cecil, chief minister. He also proclaimed that James VI of Scotland had the "undoubted right" to succeed to the English throne.

QUEEN ELIZABETH FACT FILE
- Born 1533
- The daughter of Henry VIII and Anne Boleyn
- Became Queen in 1558   • Reigned for 45 years
- Never married   • Died, aged 70

Ye Stage says: "Goodbye, Liz; hello, Jimmy!"

25th March, 1603

Roast my regalia! We're going to have a new King! People have been celebrating all night. There have been bonfires, dancing in the street and lots of wine and food was given away free; a lot of it by Catholics, who reckon that King James won't be as hard on them as Queen Elizabeth was. His mum, Mary Queen of Scots, was a Catholic and there's a rumour that his wife, Anne, is too! So after all the years of persecution, Catholics reckon they might be able to hold Mass* in church rather than in the cupboard under the stairs.

I met up with Will Shakespeare last night. He was celebrating with Ben Jonson and a tall man with a beard.

"Great news about James," he laughed. "Streaky, meet a good friend of ours. His name is Guy Fawkes."

* *Service of Communion held by Catholics.*

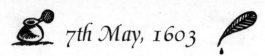

7th May, 1603

By my troth! I'm not sure about this new King of ours!

I went to see the Lord Mayor of London presenting the keys of the city to King James.

From what I saw of him he doesn't look anything special. He's not very tall, he's got bow legs and he slobbers! And he's incredibly vulgar! Not only does he pick his nose and wipe it on his sleeve, he's VERY rude!

Well really!

19th May, 1603

Pull my periwinkle! We've hit the top and no mistake!

King James has decided to be our patron. So instead of being called The Lord Chamberlain's Men, we're to become The King's Men. Alleyn, Henslowe and the Admiral's lot are spitting with jealousy, although they're allowed to carry on under the new name of The Queen's Men.

King James has said that he wants more plays at court (up to twenty a year) and guess who is going to perform the majority of them? Us!

So that'll mean lots more cash for Mr Moneybags Shakespeare!

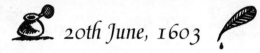

20th June, 1603

The plague's back again. The King has announced that he's going to ban all commoners from his Coronation and all the playhouses have shut down. So we're on tour again with our new play, *Measure for Measure*. Bath, Shrewsbury, Coventry and Ipswich are pencilled in – I'm tired out just thinking about it!

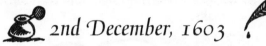

2nd December, 1603

Today, we played before King James for the first time. We were summoned to the Earl of Pembroke's house at Wilton near Salisbury and performed *As You Like It*.

Well the King must have; he's told us that we have to play at Hampton Court for the Christmas Revels (a major festive rave-up for the top bananas at court).

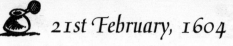

We're back in London and Will Shakespeare's moved house. He's living near Cripplegate at the house of Christopher Mountjoy, who makes tires (ridiculously expensive headdresses worn by ladies with more money than sense). Some of these wigs and hats can cost up to £50*!

I suppose it's ironic really, Mr Slaphead Shakespeare, living at a wig makers!

* *Around £30,000 at today's prices.*

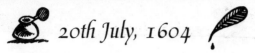

20th July, 1604

Will Shakespeare invited me up to Stratford for the summer to talk over some ideas for new plays and then let me get on with writing them! He sent me a map so I wouldn't get lost.

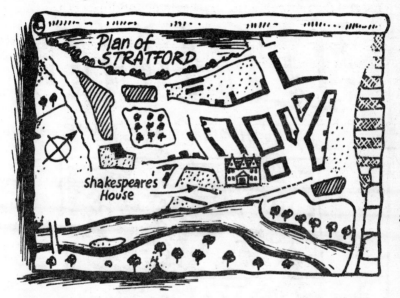

Plan of STRATFORD

Shakespeare's House

It took me a couple of days to reach Stratford. It's a small market town, surrounded by the Forest of Arden. I found his house (it's too big to miss!) and he introduced me to his wife, Anne, and his daughters, Susanna and Judith. Then he took me out walking on his new estates. He said he was thinking of opening a golf course (a game King Jimmy brought down from Scotland with him; it's getting very popular) and maybe a health club.

I looked at the hole in my stockings and thought that someone had got this entertainment business right, and it wasn't me!

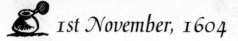

The Globe Theatre Presentes

In Cyprus, no one can hear you screame...

OTHELLO

by William Shakespeare

Played by The King's Men.

We performed *Othello* at Whitehall for the King. It went down a treat. The King has told us that we've got to perform lots of plays over the Christmas period.

This favouritism has annoyed Edward Alleyn so much that he's decided to make a farewell performance and retire (again!) to concentrate on his business. I'm sure he'll be back, he's had more comebacks than a boomerang!

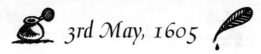

3rd May, 1605

Hoots, mon! Ben Jonson is cooling his heels in prison AGAIN. He's just written a play called *Eastward Ho!* and he thought it would be absolutely hilarious to make fun of King Jimmy's accent.

Wrong! King James sent him straight to jail. He didn't pass Go, and he didn't collect two hundred pounds, but he did have an interview with Mr Thumbscrews, and I wouldn't be surprised if he had a chat with Mr Red-hot Poker as well!

17th June, 1605

Shakespeare's got his way about writing gloomy plays. We've just finished *King Lear*. It's all about death, betrayal, madness and mutilation. "Just like life, Streaky," Shakespeare said yesterday, sighing like anything.

He's been in a very strange mood recently. Still, King James will probably lap it up, the miserable old devil.

The Globe Theatre Presentes

KING LEAR

by William Shakespeare

"I cried my eyes oute" - the Duke of Gloucester

Played by THE KING'S MEN

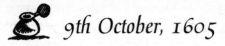

9th October, 1605

I gatecrashed a party at the Irish Boy tavern in the Strand. I went along with Will Shakespeare, Ben Jonson (who's just been let out of jail) and a few friends of theirs, including that tall man with a beard I'd met before; Guy Fawkes. I was introduced to them.

They were in a foul mood and I think I know why. Ever since the King wrote a pamphlet saying how terrible tobacco is, all cigar packets have had to carry a health warning.

HM GOVERNMENT WARNING
His Majesty King James says
Tobacco is very bad for you, the noo.

So watch out and put it out!

I must admit, I agree with the King, I hate the filthy stuff, but cigar-face Shakespeare didn't see it like that.

"First he gets at the Catholics, now this!" he wailed.

The others nodded.

"Something should be done about it!"

"Maybe something will, Will," said Robert Catesby.

I wonder what he meant by that?

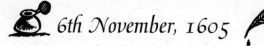 6th November, 1605

Galloping gunpowder! What is this country coming to?

YE STAGE

6th November 1605   25 groats   Ye papere for ye luvvies

PLOT TO KILL KING

Yesterday evening a wicked plot to kill the King was foiled by the guards at Westminster Palace.

A man was arrested in a cellar full of gunpowder under the palace of Westminster. He gave his name as 'John Johnson', although this is believed to be an alias. He is helping the guards with their enquiries.

In other words, he's being tortured

FIREWORKS

The King had been due to open parliament today. If the explosion had taken place, King James, Queen Anne, Prince Henry and many noble men and ladies would have died.

The King's chief minister, Henry Cecil, commented: "It has pleased God to uncover the plot."

Will Shakespeare went a funny colour when I showed him the paper. Perhaps he's relieved that the King wasn't killed. After all, we are The King's Men. What would happen to us if our patron ended up splattered all over London?

7th November, 1605

I was walking across London Bridge when I saw a crowd of people gathering round a poster.

WANTED.

Powder Plot Plotters

The man taken on the evening of the fifth of November has admitted that his real name is Guido Fawkes

The following people are also wanted

Robert Catesby   John Wright
Robert Wintour.   Thomas Wintour
Christopher Wright   Thomas Percy
Thomas Bates   Sir Everard Digby
Robert Keyes   Francis Tresham
        Ambrose Rookwood

and anybody else who looks suspicious, people you don't like, old ladies with a squint, anyone who might be a Catholic etc etc.
Any Information to The King

As I read it, I went all goosepimply.

I took the poster down and went to the Red Lion inn, where I found Will Shakespeare and Ben Jonson sitting in a corner looking worried.

I showed him the poster. "Wouldn't it be a shame," I said innocently, "if the King got to hear that Mr Shakespeare, shareholder in the King's own company of actors, is friends with Fawkes, Catesby, Rookwood, Everard and the rest of them?"

Shakespeare gave a nervous cough and looked at Jonson.

"I want a pay rise," I said. "A big one. *And* I don't want to write so many plays. *And* I get to ride on the horse when we go on tour."

Without a moment's delay he said, "Agreed."

Isn't blackmail a wonderful thing!

10th November, 1605

The news on the street is that several of the plotters have been caught and are being taken to the Tower. Some of them died while trying to fight their way to freedom. Given the choice between death and being in the Tower, I reckon the dead are the lucky ones. Dead lucky, you might say!

 31st January, 1606

YE STAGE

31st January 1606   25 groats   *Ye papere for ye luvvies*

WHAT A SHOW!

The people of London were given a wonderful treat, as the Catholic traitors who had tried to blow up the King and Parliament were sent to their doom.

Yesterday, at St Paul's churchyard, four of the Westminster Eight (Sir Everard Digby, Robert Wintour, John Grant and Thomas Bates) received their marching orders. They were HUNG, then, whilst still alive, they were CUT OPEN and their INSIDES were taken out and BURNT. Finally they were cut into QUARTERS to make sure they wouldn't do it again.

Today the same fate is in store for Tom Wintour, Ambrose Rookwood, Robert Keyes and Guy Fawkes at Westminster.

Be there early if you want a seat!

> **MAD MEG'S ASTROLOGY:**
> I see a bad time for Catholics over the next few years.

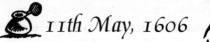

11th May, 1606

Will Shakespeare's been acting very cagily since the Powder Plot blew up (or to be more exact, didn't blow up).

He said that we needed to get back into the King's good books (I didn't think we were out of them), so my new job is to write a play about a Scottish King and make James look good in it!

The Globe Theatre Presentes

Macbeth
by William Shakespeare

She wanted it all... he committed murder for her.

He was out of his depth... She was out of her mind.

played by The King's Men

I had to do a lot of research on witches for this play. Personally, I don't believe in witches, but many people do.

Whenever anything goes wrong, like a cow gets struck by lightning or somebody gets sick, there's always some poor old woman around to take the blame. Then she gets thrown in the river, and if she drowns she's innocent (dead innocent, in fact) and if she floats they take her out and burn her. Anyway, King Jimmy believes in witchcraft (he's written a book about it*) so I've put some witches in the play to keep him happy.

* *Demonologie, written in 1597 before James came to the English throne.*

28th November, 1607

I found Will Shakespeare crying at his desk today. He told me that Edmund, his younger brother, had shuffled off his mortal coil.

"You mean Ed's dead," I said.

Shakespeare winced and nodded.

He's to be buried at St Saviour's church near the Globe. It seems appropriate as he was an actor.

He was only twenty-seven. It was the big P that got him.

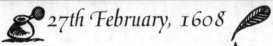
27th February, 1608

Will Shakespeare came in today hopping, jigging and skipping about.

"I'm a grandad," he shouted. "Susanna's given birth to a baby." (Well, it would have been a shock if it had been a penguin.)

His daughter, Susanna, got married to Dr John Hall last June, which means they haven't waited too long in getting down to breeding!

He showed me a picture of the slobbering kid. "She's called Elizabeth."

I must admit she looks just like Will Shakespeare...

Neither of them have got much hair.

26th March, 1608

Burst my bladder*! Interesting news this morning…

26 March 1608   25 groats   *Ye papere for ye luvvies*

KIDS KICKED OUT

The Blackfriars kids have been booted out of their theatre.

The King himself gave the order for the brats to be shown the royal red card after the cheeky chappies gave offence to his Majesty once too often.

BYE BYE BRATS

In the past the kids have been warned about

- playing plays without a licence
- Being too "political"
- making fun of Scottish accents.

Now they've insulted the French Ambassador with a play about the French King, Henry IV.

The news is that Richard Burbage's King's Men will take over the Blackfriars. *that's us!*

All this means that I've got to write some plays that can be staged outside at the Globe and indoors at the Blackfriars!
   More work!

* *A bag of air used by clowns.*

9th September, 1608

More sad news from Stratford. Will Shakespeare's mum died a couple of days ago.

2nd October, 1609

A pox on poetry! While I've been flogging myself to death writing his plays, Will Shakespeare's been writing more poems – 150 of them! Mind you, there are only fourteen lines in each one. They're called sonnets.

A lot of them seem to be about someone Shakespeare fancies, but he goes all cagey when I ask him who. It's a bit of a mystery.

One of them starts, *"Shall I compare thee to a summer's day...?"*

I suppose he means: "You're a bit wet and not very bright."

7th March, 1611

It's been a quiet time on the writing and performing fronts. Plague has meant that the theatres have been closed down yet again, and Will Shakespeare has been spending more time with his family in Stratford. I've been writing my latest play, *The Winter's Tale*, which is going to be put on at the Globe. In one bit, Shakespeare wanted a stage direction: "*Exit, pursued by a bear.*"

I said, why a bear? He said he had done a deal with the man who ran the bear-baiting* pit next door to the Globe; he could use one of the bears for his play if we put on bear-baiting at the Globe once a week.

I said he must be mad. He said the bear was going cheap. I said that was a novelty, bears usually went "growl".

7th August, 1611

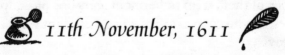

Shakespeare's cheered up a lot recently. All this time he's spending with his family must be doing him some good. Now he says we ought to write more 'family entertainment'.

"I see an island!" he shouted. "I see magicians, I see spirits, I see monsters!"

I see a lot of work...

11th November, 1611

We performed our 'family entertainment' at Whitehall for the King. It's called *The Tempest*. It went down a storm!

* A cruel sport in which dogs were set upon bears.

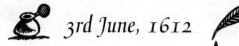

3rd June, 1612

Knock me down with a feather made of lead! Will
Shakespeare reckons that his (or rather my) playwriting
days are over!

He wandered into the Globe yesterday and showed me
a poster.

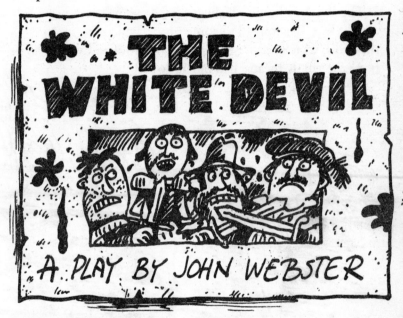

THE WHITE DEVIL

A PLAY BY JOHN WEBSTER

"This is what the people want," he said. "They don't want
a nice romantic comedy or a historical costume drama.
People want action plays. Bad dialogue, bad plots, lots of
blood and gore. And I don't want to do them. So that's it.
I'm retiring."

It took a couple of seconds for this to sink in. "You
mean *I'm* retiring?" I asked.

"Same thing. Finish off that play about Henry VIII and
that's it. I'm off to Stratford to do some gardening."

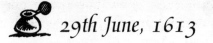 # 29th June, 1613

Burn my breeches! I've always wanted to bring the house down with a red-hot show and I have – literally!

The King's Men were performing *Henry VIII* at the Globe. Will Shakespeare had come up from Stratford to see it, still smoking his foul cigars.

The show had only just begun when some costumes caught fire. This spread to some props, which set fire to the walls, which set fire to the thatched roof and within an hour the whole theatre had burnt down!

By some miracle, nobody was hurt apart from one man whose trousers caught fire! Luckily, someone threw a mug of ale over him and put out his hot bot.

Afterwards, I asked Shakespeare, "Are you sure you stubbed out your cigar properly?"

He slipped me ten pounds to blame the fire on the cannon that announced the King's entrance.

"Don't worry," I told him, "no one will ever know the truth!"

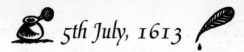

5th July, 1613

Burbage and the shareholders have decided to rebuild the Globe. They've put up nearly £1,500. The new Globe is going to be even better than the first one. It's going to have a tiled roof (and lots of No Smoking signs!).

Will Shakespeare was asked to chip in, but he said he wasn't interested. He said the new Globe "just wouldn't be the same". He hardly ever comes to London these days; he prefers to be at home in Stratford.

Henslowe and Alleyn of The Queen's Men are also building a new theatre. It's called the Hope. Dickie Burbage says he *hopes* they don't make much money!

With jokes like that, who needs Will Kemp?

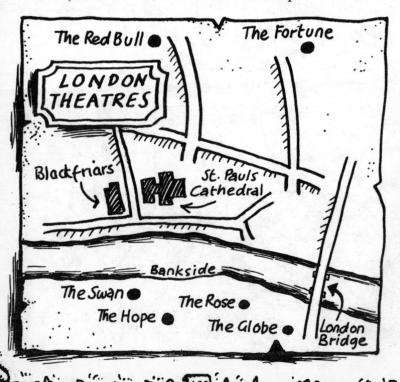

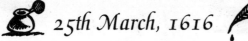

25th March, 1616

I went down to Stratford to see Will Shakespeare. He didn't look very well. He was sniffling and coughing and moaning about having a headache. He blames it on the pickled herrings and wine we had in a booze-up in London last week!

He asked me to be a witness to the signing of his will. He'd decided to change it because his daughter, Judith, married a bit of a rogue and Shakespeare wants to make sure that his new son-in-law doesn't get any of his money. Mind you, his wife must have upset him as well.

Will's Will

Judith (daughter) can have 150 pounds and some silver plate

Joan (sister) can have twenty pounds and my clothes

My fellow actors, Burbage, Heminges and Condell can have some money to buy remembrance rings.

My wife can have the second best bed and furniture

Susanna Hall (daughter) can have everything else!

Signed *William Shakespeare*

Witnessed by *Eggbert Noah Bacon*

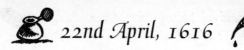

22nd April, 1616

It's Will Shakespeare's fifty-second birthday tomorrow and he's still not well. He had a fever and was lying in bed when I went round to see him this morning. I gave him a present that I'd had drawn in London. It was his family tree.

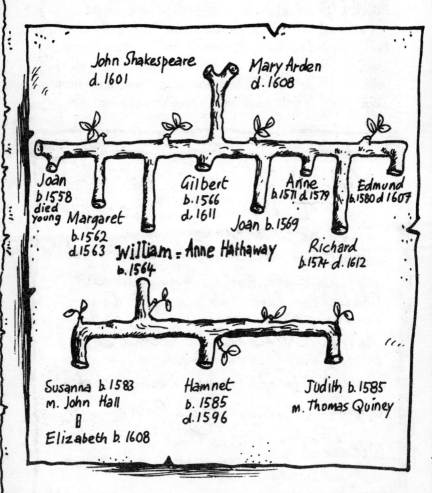

John Shakespeare d. 1601

Mary Arden d. 1608

Joan b. 1558 died young

Margaret b. 1562 d. 1563

William = Anne Hathaway b. 1564

Gilbert b. 1566 d. 1611

Joan b. 1569

Anne b. 1571 d. 1579

Edmund b. 1580 d. 1607

Richard b. 1574 d. 1612

Susanna b. 1583 m. John Hall

Elizabeth b. 1608

Hamnet b. 1585 d. 1596

Judith b. 1585 m. Thomas Quiney

"All those deaths," he murmured and then he recalled some lines from *Macbeth*, which he'd told me to write.

I left him alone with his thoughts. As I went I could hear him sniffling.

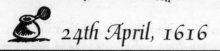

Will Shakespeare died yesterday on his fifty-second birthday. It was also St George's day, the patron saint of England.

I was called to his home by a messenger. He told me that Mr Shakespeare was very ill and wanted to speak to me.

I arrived at New Place and went into his bedroom. Will Shakespeare was lying in bed with his eyes half-closed. His wife, daughters and John Hall were at his bedside. They were crying.

He must have heard me come in. "Ah, Streaky," he wheezed, "I want you to write something down for me."

Always had to have the last word, didn't he! I picked up a paper and quill from a table.

"Ready?" he asked.

I nodded yes.

And with his last breath, William Shakespeare whispered his final line:

THE FINAL CURTAIN

William Shakespeare was buried in front of the altar of Stratford church on 25th April, 1616.

His wife, Anne, died in 1623, the same year that Shakespeare's plays were published. His friends, John Heminges and Henry Condell, collected together all The King's Men's scripts and playbooks. From this material, they published the first official collection of Shakespeare's plays. This was called the *First Folio* and consisted of thirty-six plays. Just over 200 copies of the *First Folio* still exist.

In the years that followed, it was gradually recognised that Shakespeare had written the greatest collection of plays the world had ever seen.

HISTORICAL NOTE: BY R. CELAVIE, PROFESSOR OF HISTORY
at Trinity College, Basingstoke

There have been several attempts to prove that 'Shakespeare's plays' were not written by William Shakespeare.

This book's claim that Barlow and Skidmore have solved this age-old mystery must be treated with extreme caution!

There is no general agreement as to the exact dates of the plays; the dating given in this 'Lost Diary' is in line with most authorities, as are the basic historical facts.

However, there are a number of 'minor' lapses of historical accuracy in the book:

• No newspaper called *Ye Stage* existed in the sixteenth and seventeenth centuries.

• There would have been no sense in Eggbert's doctor asking whether he was a 'private' patient as there was no National Health Service in Elizabethan times – and no health insurance companies, either.

• Although the Globe did burn down during a performance of Henry VIII, this was caused by some wadding from a cannon shot and not by a cigar. Indeed, cigars were not in existence in Shakespeare's time.

As to who really wrote Shakespeare's plays, various suggestions have been made over the years. These include:

• Christopher Marlowe (who, according to the theory, survived being stabbed through the brain in 1593)

• Sir Francis Bacon (Streaky's half-brother according to Barlow and Skidmore!)

• The Earl of Oxford.

However, there is no reliable evidence to support any of these claims, all of which are based on the idea that Shakespeare can't have been a great playwright because he only went to grammar school, while real gentlemen went to public school.

These arguments are based on ignorance, prejudice and hogwash. The so-called 'evidence' of this 'Lost Diary' notwithstanding, there is no sensible reason to suppose that Shakespeare's plays were written by anyone other than... William Shakespeare!

Order Form

To order direct from the publishers, just make a list of the titles you want and fill in the form below:

Name ....

Address ....

....

....

Send to: Dept 6, HarperCollins Publishers Ltd, Westerhill Road, Bishopbriggs, Glasgow G64 2QT.

Please enclose a cheque or postal order to the value of the cover price, plus:

UK & BFPO: Add £1.00 for the first book, and 25p per copy for each additional book ordered.

Overseas and Eire: Add £2.95 service charge. Books will be sent by surface mail but quotes for airmail despatch will be given on request.

A 24-hour telephone ordering service is available to holders of Visa, MasterCard, Amex or Switch cards on 0141- 772 2281.

Collins
An *Imprint* of HarperCollins*Publishers*